West End Story

By

John F King

ISBN 9780993130656

2017

Dramatis Personae>

Carstairs

Edward Carstairs is Britain's leading playwright. His early writings for stage were so successful he left Oxford Univ without graduating. He has been the dominating force in London West End drama as long as he can remember. His writing has made him, and many others, rich. In the mid 1970s as fashions change around him can he change with the times too? Does he know he needs to?

XS

Lady Xavier Sinclair is one of the grand dames of British theatre. She has been long associated with the work of Edward Carstairs, she has been long associated with Carstairs himself, although their relationship has been described in some of the less deferential newspapers as ' on – off'. Though successful she remains ambitious and wary of stereotyping. This may make her seem ruthless but those who criticise Carstairs to her may find it has unexpected consequences.

Sir

Sir Antony Wolf is a star of stage, and if lucrative enough screen. TW is competent and loyal and professional. In the West End it is easier just to call him Sir

Brian Anderson

'No one ever erected a statue to a critic' - yet.

Pheobe Grace

In mid 1970s London music, not theatre, is where it's at for young people. So why is this young woman wasting her time riding around on buses taking notes on life around her?

Archie

The enigmatic doorman at the Apollo theatre seems to have been around for ever. But he hasn't. How does he know everything about theatre?

Y

Y is musician in a punk band. That way round. And she can act, speak, compose proper music…

Lionel

Lionel is director of the Royal Court Theatre, he successfully stops happening things happening

Garrick club porter, door and bar,

Bus conductor, BBC presenter, cabbie

Time: mid-1970s… / Place: London

A sound story / JK 2017

1- EVENING INT

PERFORMANCE ON STAGE APOLLO THEATRE

XS ' Life is but a series of moments. It doesn't have to add up, it may only make sense with hindsight. You may have many luxuries. But not that one.

SIR Hindsight is for dead people. I've never felt more alive. More sure.

XS This time isn't going to come again.

SIR You think waiting is a fashion, darling. That went out with ocean liners, with…

XS This time isn't going to come again.

SIR From this moment onward, there is only one time…

XS One time, darling?

SIR Our time. Our perpetual present. Our time.'

HE PUTS DOWN GLASS, CROSSES BOARDS AND KISSES XS. CURTAIN. A BRIEF PAUSE IN THE AUDITORIUM.

BRI IN THE AUDITORIUM, SOTTO VOCE My God, Carstairs you bastard, you've…

SILENCE BREAKS, THE APPLAUSE STARTS BUILDS,

CRESCENDO, OVATIONS, SHOUTS OF 'Bravo'

BRI You've done it again

THE APPLAUSE CONTINUES, NO SIGN OF DYING, BRIAN IN FOYER DIALLING, INTO TELEPHONE

BRI The West End star that is Edward Carstairs shows no signs of waning. Indeed it is those who seek to write him off into the wings of theatrical history that may find it is themselves who are written off. It looks, sounds, feels as if Apollo has once again found a hit on its books. If it ain't broke don't fix it. The touch is sure, the tone deft, the applause never ending…I said the tone is deft, the applause ….

ARCHIE AT STAGE DOOR, THE APPLAUSE STILL AUDIBLE You are not staying for the curtain call, Mr Carstairs?

CARSTAIRS No time, Archie old son, bar will be closed by time that applause dies down

ARCHIE I'm sure you know more about these things than I do, Mr Carstairs

CARSTAIRS Closing time?

ARCHIE Applause, sir

CARSTAIRS I've told you before Archie, I was never knighted.

ARCHIE Allow me to voice what a pleasure it is to have you back in the house.

Lovely to have the applause ringing through the old place again. Glad to have rid of that filth flop we had on last week.

CARSTAIRS A long run then, Archie. Right theatre, wrong play or variant thereof. I believe it is what is called in some quarters experimental.

ARCHIE Knew you would have the right word for it Mr Carstairs. Goodnight to you sir. Edward.

2 INT/ EXT ACOUSTIC THE SOUND OF THE APPLAUSE FADES AS CARSTAIRS EMERGES ONTO BUSTLING SHAFTESBURY AVENUE. BUSY WITH BUSES, TAXIS, THEATRE GOERS EMERGING FROM OTHER THEATRES.

CARSTAIRS PAUSES TO LIGHT CIGARETTE AND BEGINS TO WALK DOWN THE AVENUE. WHISTLES A FEW BARS TO HIMSELF OF 'A NIGHTINGALE SANG IN BERKELEY SQUARE.'

CARSTAIRS A spring night, London, West London, Shaftesbury Avenue. A May night, a first night, hardly dawn, certainly bliss. What could be merrier? Conversely what could be darker than a grand theatre going dark . I do hope I have really delivered another hit for the Apollo. Not for my sake of course – do I need it - but for those who love theatre, depend on it, live for it, live off it. I must say they did make some rather odd programming choices. I mean look at all the other theatres on the Avenue:

CARSTAIRS READS REVIEW A-BOARDS OUTSIDE OTHER SHAFTESBURY AVENUE THEATRES, ALL SHOWING HIS PLAYS

CARSTAIRS Lyric : 'Lilac in Spring'– 'it's that man again, Carstairs' 'the man for whom there is no Autumn' – who writes this stuff? Globe: Five stars for 'The Sun Revolves Around You' ' the searing drama you have to see.' Critics , zeugma and failed alliteration. What does one expect? Queen's: Curtains for the Drawing Room, 'a lesson in how to fill a theatre' – curiously phrased, yes one of Brian's signature critiques, the bastard as Janus. Critics, who cares about those who only write about. HE OVERHEARS COMMENTS OF THEATRE GOERS THRONGING ONTO THE STREET:

'absolutely marvellous' 'loved every minute, except for that dreadful plonk they serve at half time' 'splendid' 'I could do with another drink'

'do you think they might be, you know, samey. Complacent..?' 'Yes, next time we could try something new.' 'why risk failure, I want a good night out, top show, topped off by supper, speaking of which…'

CARSTAIRS WALKS ON, SILENT, LIGHTS ANOTHER CIGARETTE AMONG THE THRONG, CROSSING NEAR LEICESTER SQUARE HE HEARS VERY LOUD PUNK MUSIC COMING FROM A CLUB.

CARSTAIRS Extraordinary. I've never heard anything like it. Extraordinary.

HE IS TRANSFIXED, THEN CONTINUES TO GARRICK CLUB

DOORMAN May I congratulate you on behalf of the Garrick Club, sir?

CARSTAIRS Have the first editions arrived yet?

DOOR Presently, I believe, sir.

CARSTAIRS Then what are you congratulating me upon?

DOOR Another successful opening, sir. Word travels faster than print. The papers will be in the library imminently. Any newspaper in particular we should bring to you?

HE ENTERS THE CLUB BAR

BARMAN Your usual, sir?

CARSTAIRS Yes, I mean no, what are young people drinking these days?

BARMAN A lager, Mr Carstairs, are you sure?

AS HE POURS THE DRINK THERE IS A COMMOTION OUTSIDE

DOOR Madam, please. This area of the club is gentlemen only.

XS Do you know who I am?

DOOR I regret Lady Sinclair. This area of the club is gentlemen only. I don't make the rules.

XS It is imperative I see Edward- Mr Carstairs - immediately

DOOR I can take a message of course madam.

XS This is something that can only be said face to face. I doubt he would appreciate a public performance of my message. I must insist…

THE COMMOTION CONTINUES BUT EVENTUALLY SUBSIDES

CARSTAIRS Is everything alright outside?

BARMAN A minor fracas at the door sir, involving a woman I believe. Shall I refill your schooner sir?

CARSTAIRS Yes, I mean no, perhaps I will have the usual.

TELEPHONE RINGS

BARMAN Are you in, sir?

CARSTAIRS Who?

BARMAN Gentleman, sir. No name, no manners. Insistent type.

PASSING PHONE TO CARSTAIRS

CARSTAIRS A gentleman you say. I was rather hoping….ON TELEHONE Carstairs, good evening.

BRI Evening Carstairs.

CARSTAIRS Brian, Have you been drinking?

BRI Enough. Look Carstairs, nothing personal, thought it only sporting to let you know. I'm going to ruin you. Down the hatch.

PHONE BACK TO DIALLING TONE. CARSTAIRS HANDS PHONE SET BACK TO BARMAN.

BARMAN Everything hunky dory, sir?

CARSTAIRS Someone's had a drop too much lager, I surmise. Usual usual. Please

DOORMAN ENTERS WITH MESSAGE WHICH HE GIVES TO BARMAN.

A message for Mr Carstairs.

BARMAN My domain. I'll deal with it.

HE SERVES THE DRINK TO CARSTAIRS.

TO CARSTAIRS A message for you, sir.

CARSTAIRS Read it would you, my good man. I'm busy drinking right now.

BARMAN As you wish, sir. It's from Lady Sinclair. I quote: I'm leaving you. End of quote.

CARSTAIRS You read that rather well you know, a trifle melodramatic, but we can't help the lines we are given I surmise.

LATER THAT SAME NIGHT , IN THE STREET OUTSIDE THE CLUB- EXT ACOUSTIC

DOOR I'll call you a cab, sir

CARSTAIRS ATTEMPTING THE OLD JOKE - a cab sir

DOOR Quite, sir. WHISTLES FOR CAB. TO CARSTAIRS Usual sir?

TO CABBIE Highgate.

INSIDE THE CAB THROUGH NORTH LONDON AT NIGHT,

CABBIE'S MONOLOGUE

CABBIE …Country going to ruin, Labour Govt, them Sex pistols, -PASSING CAMDEN Camden, litter, National service, IRA, EEC…

Excuse me Guv, you're not taking notes are you. Have I seen you on the radio?

CARSTAIRS EXT / INT ACOUSTIC, OUT OF CAB, UNLOCKING FRONT DOOR

Darling, I'm home. Darling?

3 - DAY INT/ EXT ACOUSTIC STREET TO TOP DECK OF LONDON TRANSPORT ROUTEMASTER EN ROUTE PECKHAM TO CENTRAL LONDON

PHEOBE Buses are my libraries, my locations, my limo. Look, listen, learn. Hold tight, sit tight, look. Top deck, observation deck. Look before you write. It's all there. I've always seen it. Don't know why. I wasn't that clever at school. Failed my 11 plus. Guess exams and me are strangers, they make me feel like a loser. I was unemployed when I left school. Listened to the radio. Moved the dial around. Music, words, windows. Works for me.

Look at that. Man smoking, derelict shop window, used to be a record store, maybe he owned it, maybe he was in a band in the sixties, charted big time, now look at him, how did he get from there to here, what's the arc? Yeah, I know about arcs, class at the library, loving it.

Look at that. Woman pushing a pram with three wheels, what's the story there, is the dad pushing another pram with one wheel? Look at that...

CONDUCTOR Fares please. Where to, Young lady? I said where to, young lady, you're in another world.

PHEOBE Sloane Square

CONDUCTOR Sloane Square indeed, you're crossing a river there. Buying a new outfit are we?

PHEOBE You think I need one? New life maybe.

CONDUCTOR First day at work? Secretary?

PHEOBE Why do you think that?

CONDUCTOR Notebook. Write fast. Indecipherable.

PHEOBE Nice story, bus crossing river, conductor thinks it's your first day at work as a secretary but you are really a wri...

CONDUCTOR I haven't time for life stories. I can tell you where to get off, if you haven't been north of the river before. ISSUES TICKET AND MOVES ON fares please.

THE BUS CONTINUES, PHEOBE CONTINUES TAKING NOTES

CONDUCTOR You never stop writing do you and I doubt it is bus numbers. This is it. Peter Jones, Holy Trinity Church, Venus Fountain, Royal Court on left, darling.

PHEOBE How did you…Thank you, you know I've got an idea for a play, would you mind if…

THE BUS DRIVES ON, PHEOBE CLIMBS STEPS, OPENS SWING DOORS

EXT – INT ACOUSTIC UP MORE STAIRS INTO A REHEARSAL ROOM

LIONEL Miss Grace, thank you for coming in. How was your journey?

4 - EVENING INT BRIAN'S TOP FLOOR FLAT IN THE LONDON TRELLICK TOWER

BRIAN AND XS AIR KISS THEATRICALLY

BRI Thank you for coming, darling. Do you mind if I call you by your real name?

XS Keep it professional

HE WANTS TO TAKE THEATRICAL KISS FURTHER.

XS I think this is the scene when you offer me a drink.

BRI After

XS You have a layman's sense of sequences.

BRI This isn't a play

XS Are you sure. What would you know. You are only a critic. Sorry.

BRI Something on the rocks, I presume. HE MIXES DRINKS, XS CROSSES TO WINDOWS.

XS Trellick Tower. Quite a view, for a council house.

BRI I'm not looking out of the windows

XS Say what you have to say, why am I here?

BRI After

XS I don't have time for this. I don't care what floor you live on or who designed your flat. You think scenery impresses actresses?

BRI Fine, we'll sequence it your way.

HE OPENS A NEWSPAPER First edition proof. This is for your eyes only. Until it hits the streets, railway stations, radio stations, television channel early. HE READS

Politics, music, fashion, lapels and hemlines, everything goes in cycles, It's the Law. Spengler, Toynbee, knew it. Nothing is exempt. Not even West End theatre, not even Edward Carstairs. The end is nigh. Unless two things happen, one I'm wrong, or two Carstairs does something new. Nothing, no one, is exempt from the law. Readers will of course be cognisant of the splendid Spenglerian sociology of fossilisation. I hardly need explain it. Some readers may be surprised to read that I am predicting, indeed announcing the end of the Carstairs era. Mr Carstairs currently has 3 productions running on Shaftesbury Avenue, all to full houses, and I write as the previews of his latest production promise more of the same – full houses. But it is, to revert to Spenglerian theory the last season. Only this is not theory. Mr Carstairs is a dinosaur, no one would dare challenge the dinosaurs at their zenith but after a zenith comes extinction, and the dinosaurs, unchallenged for so long were the last to know. The curtains will fall on the proscenium arch, the drawing room set, the ABC dialogue, the arch creation and solution of tidily messy romances. This morning I announce the ashes of Mr Carstairs aptly named West End, and a new day of brave new writing, perhaps not as opulently crafted as the writings of Edward Carstairs but writing on walls is a different skill, one into which he and his species will be unable to evolve into as new forms, at one lighter and darker will advance through London, from south to north, east to west, capital to provinces, new subjects, new people, a new era, an era which starts today, an era which you read here first before you could see it.'

What do you think. Darling. Of course the night is still young, the presses are hot but not rolling, yet. Darling.

XS How dare you? How dare you call that writing? How dare you call me darling. And you mix drinks as dreadfully as your metaphors. I wouldn't even throw this over you.

SHE SLAMS DOWN DRINK AND WALKS OUT TO THE LIFT

5 – DAY INT THE ROYAL COURT REHEARSAL ROOM

PHEOBE My journey in was fine, how was yours?

LIONEL, DIRECTOR First, welcome to the Royal Court, we hope you will feel at home in our house, second let me introduce you to two other members of our commissioning panel, Sir and XS. I'm sure you will have heard of them.

PHEOBE No

LIONEL Look, there is no point beating about the Bush Theatre. I'm sure you are very busy.

PHEOBE I have time for the right things, right people, right places.

LIONEL Quite, as I said no point …

PHEOBE I haven't taken my writing to any other theatres if that is what you are trying to say.

LIONEL Let me put it this way. You have no sense of plot or character development, no ear for dialogue, no concept of theatrical denouement, no…However, we would like to ….I'm sorry , perhaps you would like to make a comment, Pheobe, if I may.

PHEOBE Does your budget run to my bus fare home?

LIONEL Right, so that's the positives, let's listen to some dialogue. XS, Sir, in your own time:

THEY READ FROM CARSTAIRS OPENING SCENE

XS Life is but a series of moments. It doesn't have to add up, it may only make sense with hindsight. You may have many luxuries. But not that one.

SIR Hindsight is for dead people. I've never felt more alive. More sure.

XS This time isn't going to come again.

SIR You think waiting is a fashion, darling. That went out with ocean liners, with…

XS This time isn't going to come again.

SIR From this moment onward, there is only one time…

XS One time, darling?

SIR Our time. Our perpetual present. Our time.

LIONEL Thank you. Miss Grace, if you - and we will support you in your work – rewrite some of the dialogue of some of the scenes you have submitted to us The Royal Court as Britain's premier venue for new writing would be keen to develop your voice, your work for the future. Premiere in our One to Watch programme. What do you say, any questions?

PHEOBE Interesting you talk of dialogue but you don't listen.

LIONEL I'm sorry?

SIR I'm not sure you realise what the director…

XS What the theatre…

SIR Is offering you.

PHEOBE You asked me if I have any questions but you didn't answer my last one

You asked me here, does your budget run to my bus fare home?

SHE IS LEAVING

XS Do something, she thinks rewrite is a rejection

SIR Don't just sit there, man. Bring the future back

LIONEL CALLING AFTER PHEOBE AS SHE EXITS STAGE DOOR STAIRS

Call me, my number is on the front of the theatre.

HE RETURNS

SIR What did she say, man?

LIONEL We can't use that sort of language in the theatre.

EXT ACOUSTIC, IN FRONT OF THE THEATRE SLOANE SQUARE

BUS SLOWS BUT DOESN'T ENTIRELY STOP AS PHEOBE BOARDS MOVING ROUTEMASTER. SAME CONDUCTOR AS HER OUTWARD JOURNEY

CONDUCTOR I'd prefer it if you would board at a recognised bus stop. You.

Of course. A theatrical entrance. Hold tight please.

PHEOBE Not the most original of lines.

CONDUCTOR Terminus

PHEOBE How did you know?

CONDUCTOR Thought you'd be going home in a Daimler, young lady.

SHE PAYS FARE, HE ISSUES TICKET, SILENCE BETWEEN

THEM AS BUS MOVES OFF AND SHE RESUMES WRITING IN HER NOTEBOOK

PHEOBE IN NOTEBOOK

The river, a border of water, invisible borders can be the hardest to scale…

CONDUCTOR So?

PHEOBE So what? I'm working, why aren't you?

CONDUCTOR So how did it go, darling

PHEOBE Don't you darling me.

CONDUCTOR Listen , darling, you don't have to be rude just because you're…

PHEOBE What?

CONDUCTOR Just because you're a writer. Hold tight please.

6 - DAY / EVENING INT

TAXI EN ROUTE THROUGH NORTH LONDON TO WEST END

SAME TAXI DRIVER AS BEFORE, IN FULL FLOW

CARSTAIRS Shaftesbury Avenue, my good man

CABBIE EEC , PM, Lefties, Trade Unions, Play for Today, had to turn it off, filth, wouldn't let the wife watch it, Punks…

ARRIVING AT THE THEATRE

CARSTAIRS Keep the change.

CABBIE Thank you, sir. You're a real gentlemen. Not so many on this street these days, I shouldn't wonder.

CARSTAIRS What do you mean, on this street, these days?

CABBIE No offence, guv. You're a real gent. Theatrical type, methinks. Look let me give you a tip, gratis, for nothing.

CARSTAIRS By all means.

CABBIE Drop the 'my good man' guff. Makes you sound dated. Not my line of work 'course but all the worlds a stage and all that. Only trying to be helpful.

BRI This taxi free? Carstairs old man.

CARSTAIRS Brian, what are you doing this neck of the street?

BRIAN ENTERS CAB. CABBIE REPEATS BACK BRIAN'S REQUEST

CABBIE South of the river, squire. You sure?

BRI FROM CAB WINDOW TO CARSTAIRS

It isn't where you've been, it's where you are going, old fellow.

TAXI DRIVES OFF QUICKLY

EXT – INT ACOUSTIC AS CARSTAIRS ENTERS THEATRE

CARSTAIRS Good evening, Archie old son.

ARCHIE Good Evening, Mr Carstairs sir.

CARSTAIRS All right Archie, what's going on?

ARCHIE Going on sir?

CARSTAIRS Archie, you live on Shaftesbury Avenue. If you don't know what is going on it isn't going on.

Not the usual buzz about the place. What is going on? What is it? Critics got to you first?

OFFERS HIM A TENNER

ARCHIE I don't want you to give me anything, sir. Anyway I've got my hands full already. Louts, punks, leafleting the street, they call it publicity, I call it litter. Looks like filth to me sir, problem is soon as I clear one lot, another lot pop up. Proper plague it is sir. If these people have their way it'll be dead end not west end.

CARSTAIRS Don't concern yourself Archie. Here let me have a look.

HE READS FROM A FLYER

The Concrete River. A Sensational new play from a sensational new writer. Life in Britain's biggest city, see it, hear it, feel it, live it. You think theatre has no future? It's here now. Pheobe Grace had the guts to write it, have the guts to see it?

CARSTAIRS HANDS FLYER BACK TO ARCHIE

There's no business like showbusiness.

7 - EVENING EXT UNDISCLOSED VENUE IN SOUTH LONDON. EXTREMELY LOUD PUNK MUSIC, HIP BUZZ

TAXI ARRIVES, CABBIE CONTINUING USUAL ANTI CALLAGHAN, ANTI EEC, ANTI TRADE UNION, PRO ENOCH ,PRO that whatd'ya call her Iron Lady MONOLOGUE, SLIGHTLY MODIFIES THIS AS HE SEES BRI NOT AS ANTI PUNK AS HE IS, MUSIC INTENSIFIES AS CAB DOOR OPENS

CABBIE You sure this is where you want to be sir, it isn't in The Knowledge

BRI This is exactly where I want to be.

CABBIE I can keep the meter running, I mean hang around, safety precaution of course.

BRI Keep the change, young man

BRI LEAVES THE TAXI, IT DRIVES BACK QUICKLY

EXT - INT ACOUSTIC, HE OPENS THE VENUE DOOR, ENGULFED IN THE SEX PISTOLS/ CLASH /THE SLITS MUSIC

SUDDEN SILENCE, THEN NOISE OF FLOODLIGHTS, THEN DIALOGUE OF PLAY OPENING SCENE NARRATED IN READ THROUGH BY PHEOBE IN ATMOSPHERE VERY DIFFERENT TO THAT OF THE APOLLO THEATRE E.G. SHOUTS OF 'Get on with it, geroff' etc.

PHEOBE NARRATES Scene 1: the present, a block of flats off the Westway, afternoon

PHEOBE AS CHARACTER X Why don't you do something?

Y I am. To you. Like this.

X We can't do this all day , every day, forever.

Y Why not?

X Because

Y I'm waiting

X For what?

Y A reason

X You'll be waiting a long time

Y I have time. We have time.

X Fancy a smoke?

Y I'm giving up.

X I'm starting.

Y Why don't you do something?

X You've already said that

Y I mean it.

X What do you want me to do?

Y Get a job

X There aren't any.

Y Start something.

X I've started smoking. What else can I do. Start a fire?

Y Start a band. Take me places.

X I can't play. I don't know where to go.

Y All you need

X is love

Y All you need to do is start

X It's too early, it's too late, it's…

PHEOBE AS NARRATOR And they kiss

SILENCE HAS DESCENDED ON THE PERFORMANCE

BRIAN Extraodinary, extraordinary

THE APPLAUSE STARTS, LOUD MUSIC RESUMES AND FADES INTO CHAMBER MUSIC SIGNATURE THEME OF CRITICS' FORUM.

8 – DAY INT BBC RADIO 3 STUDIO LONDON AS CRITICS' FORUM IS ABOUT TO GO ON AIR. BRIAN AND CARSTAIRS ARE ON THE PANEL THEY EXCHANGE WORDS BEFORE THE THEME TUNE STOPS AND THEY ARE ON AIR

CARSTAIRS I wasn't informed you would be on the panel

BRI Problem?

CARSTAIRS Not for me. Only I wouldn't want you to be out of your depth.

BRI I wouldn't want you to be out of your comfort zone.

CARSTAIRS Meaning?

BRI I understand this is a programme covering what's new, happening, au courant. What did you understand? Down the hatchet, old man.

CARSTAIRS If I wasn't so busy being successful I might apply myself to figuring out your problem. Other than drink and being third rate and unoriginal and

BRI You calling me unoriginal. There must be an expression for that.

PRESENTER Good evening , welcome to this edition of Critics' Forum, live here on BBC Radio 3. Our studio is graced with our special guests playwright Edward Carstairs, his new play

BRI New. Excuse me

PRESENTER Our studio is graced with our special guests playwright Edward Carstairs, his new play, as yet untitled, is about to open in the West End. From the emerging world of – it says here Punk, yes Punk we have Y, her band is part of the performing arts scene in London and the Provinces

Y That's not a bad name that, London and the Provinces, mind if we use it?

PRESENTER From the Royal Court Theatre we have Lionel Smart, Good evening

LIONEL Hi

PRESENTER And in a technical marvel for these tumultuous times, we have a live audio link to the Shaftesbury Avenue of actors 'Sir' Tony Wolf and Lady Xavier Sinclair, who will be leading in Mr Carstairs new play

We'll start with the music scene. I'm so sorry. Last but not least our panel is completed this evening by a gentleman who is no stranger to London's green rooms, critic Brian Anderson

BRIAN None taken

PRESENTER We'll start with the music scene. Y

TO Y Can you explain to us the CHECKS NOTES FOR RIGHT TERM Punk phenomenon.

Y No

PRESENTER I'm sorry

Y Why do you keep saying I'm sorry?

PRESENTER You are young, I thought you would be able to explain the punk music phenomenon to or for us.

Y You are old. I can't explain anything. I don't want to explain anything.

PRESENTER I'm sorry…

CARSTAIRS Perhaps I could assist.

BRI Now that would be a phenomenon. Edward 'Fossil' Carstairs, explains punk. Did you ask dinosaurs to explain extinction?

Y TO BRI You're rude, man

BRI I'm rude?

Y Yeah man, you're rude. I'm direct. You don't know the difference. Is this radio 1 or 3?

PRESENTER Edward Carstairs, if you could assist us with a definition of punk we would be most…

Y Why do you want to define it?

CARSTAIRS I think the young lady makes an excellent point. Why define it? It seems like something you feel.

BRI Now I've heard everything, Carstairs explains punk, Carstairs explains feeling. For Fu…

PRESENTER Gentlemen, please. Edward Carstairs.

CARSTAIRS I was strolling up Shaftesbury Avenue one evening after the preview night of one of my plays when

BRI So it's all about Edward Carstairs, might have surmised.

PRESENTER Mr Anderson, you know no one has been actually asked to leave a Critics' Forum Panel live on air but in your case I wouldn't be averse to a premiere

Y Nice one, man.

CARSTAIRS When I was crossing from Shaftesbury Avenue flaneuring towards the Garrick I heard music all around me. Strange music, visceral music, music I had never heard before. A May evening, a London evening, theatre, music, bliss

BRI Excuse me while…

CARSTAIRS Bliss to hear such music of power, feeling, unrefined, unfiltered, new

BRI New! Carstairs! Same sentence?

Y Shut up, man or I'll

PRESENTER Mr Carstairs

Y Yeah, let the old guy speak, he seems to have a way with words

CARSTAIRS I was transfixed. Listening. A sound, unrefined, uncrafted, yes, but expressive, moving, as English as paddling on the beach with a handkerchief on your head.

LIONEL Did you enter the club, where the sound was emanating?

CARSTAIRS No

LIONEL You should

CARSTAIRS The director of the Royal Court is telling me what I should do? I could fill your theatre every night from now until the end of time.

LIONEL Your point?

CARSTAIRS Yours?

LIONEL Let me put this to you as a question

PRESENTER I'll ask the questions

LIONEL How do you keep up to date, I mean with what is going on

Y And this is British Theatre today? No future. Future is in music

LIONEL Could be in both

Y Could. Doesn't sound like it. I hear same people arguing over same things. You know I'm going to split. Got better things to do than talk.

BRI Yeah, me too.

Y You man, you're a destroyer

BRI Thank you

Y (LEAVING THE STUDIO TO PRESENTER STILL ON AIR)You want to know the future of theatre gents, if it is going to have one at all, two words

PRESENTER Please…

Y Phoebe Grace

Y AND BRI LEAVE , MICROPHONES REMOVED

PRESENTER Moving on, Edward Carstairs…

LIONEL (MUSING) Pheobe Grace..

PRESENTER Edward Carstairs. Your new play for the Apollo, there now follows a synopsis for our listeners:

Let's go live to the future of British theatre, and I mean the immediate future, Sir and XS in the dressing room of the Apollo theatre.

CARSTAIRS I wasn't informed you had a link to XS

BRI (PARTING SHOT) Not very well informed at all I'd say Carstairs. Pattern?

SIR Edward Carstairs is one of this country's preeminent playwrights. Perhaps Shaftesbury Avenue should be renamed Carstairs Street. His latest play is another West End sure fire hit . It tells the story of a leading London writer and an actress who has graced so many of his productions, indeed the plays are written for her and about her. There are parallels between real life and dramatic life or is that vice versa. The play is set in present day London, Holland

Park to be precise, the drawing room windows are open on a May evening, a nightingale singing in the near distance.

LIONEL Original

SIR Do I hear a sneering voice, how familiar.

PRESENTER Do please continue, sir

SIR The lead character, my character, asks the leading lady, XS, if she has any regrets. I f you could live your life over again is there anything you would do differently. She looks back on her life from the present, perhaps she has as much time in front of her, life to be lived as time she has lived. She is startled by the question, life is for her as a woman, as an actress a straight line moving forward. Perhaps some early struggles but life is a triumph. An incident, a stranger, cause her to question her personal and professional life. She embarks on a new journey, new experiences but in the end, literally at the end of the day, she arrives at the belief that

CARSTAIRS You really do need to see this play for yourselves.

PRESENTER I invited Mr Anderson, Y here to give their reviews from the previews and press night. Unfortunately they are no longer with us, in the studio. XS speculation must arise, does it not, that in some ways this drama is for you autobiographical.

XS (BY LINK) It is in no way biographical.

PRESENTER Why would you say that?

LIONEL Indeed it does seem somewhat self evident.

XS I will show not tell you why that is not self evident, gentlemen. I will not be going on.

PRESENTER Excuse me?

XS I will not be going on. Good evening. (THERE IS A RUSTLE AS SHE DISCONNECTS HER MICROPHONE)

CARSTAIRS, SIR Darling?

PRESENTER XS? I am sorry we seem to have lost the link. Edward Carstairs, can you enlighten us, does life imitate art?

CARSTAIRS I am frightfully sorry, I have to depart for the theatre immediately.

PRESENTER Mr Carstairs. Please. CARSTAIRS IS LEAVING. HE TURNS TO LIONEL What are your comments on this?

LIONEL Are you asking me as director of the Royal Court or because I appear to be the last player in the studio? Quite a performance.

9 INT – EXT ACOUSTIC CARSTAIRS ON STREET IN FRONT OF BBC HAILING CAB

CARSTAIRS Apollo, Shaftesbury Avenue, quickly as possible if you please. My good…

CABBIE (BY NOW USUAL SPIEL) Did you see that play for today on the beeb last night, wife nearly ill, don't know what is happening to this country, have you heard what they call music now, ban the lot, national service..

CARSTAIRS I don't mean to be rude it really is rather important I get to the theatre on time, could you focus on the driving?

CABBIE Get me to the theatre on time. Doesn't have write the same ring to it. Mind you,marriage, young people nowadays…

CARSTAIRS (EXPLODES) Please. I'm sorry. For being theatrical. Please. Drive.

TAXI ARRIVES AT THEATRE, CARSTAIRS EXITS CAB AND ENTERS THEATRE, DASHING UPSTAIRS FROM STAGE DOOR TOWARDS DRESSING ROOMS

ARCHIE Good Evening Mr Carstairs sir, I think you should know in advance…

CARSTAIRS Not now, Archie

ARCHIE I need to speak with you….

CARSTAIRS REACHES THE DRESSING ROOM, TO SIR

SIR You might find you are about 20 years too late old boy. I did try to talk to her

CARSTAIRS Where is she?

SIR Centre stage.

CARSTAIRS DASHES ON REACHES WINGS AS CURTAIN OPENS. XS TAKES CENTRE STAGE. APPLAUSE.

XS That is most kind. Most kind. Kinder than I deserve, if you will indulge me for a few moments…thank you, thank you. Ladies and Gentlemen. It has been, it is, my honour and privilege to grace, I should say, appear, on this stage before you, night after night, indeed year after year. The theatre is my life, the theatre gives me life, I hope I have , in my own way, through my own art, managed to convey some of the magic of theatre, of imagination, of transportation to you, my friends, the individuals who compose the audience, the faithful.

SHOUTS OF 'HEAR, HEAR, LONG MAY IT CONTINUE..'

CARSTAIRS IN THE WINGS SOTTO VOCE TO XS Darling, XS, can we talk. Now.

XS FULL FLOW CENTRE STAGE Friends, I will be candid with you. My last performance in this theatre will not be tonight, unless you regard this as a performance, My last performance in this theatre was last night. I will not be going on. I will not be going on because there is no where to go from here, in this form, in this vein, in this mode. It has all been done and said. It is time for a brave new world. I believe Mr Edward Carstairs is in the house tonight. I am glad of the opportunity to thank him, for all he has given me as an actor, for all he has given to theatre, but he is the past. I want no further ado with the past, past forms, past words, past themes, past masters. On with the new, new writing, new roles, emerging, evolving, a new age. It is time to make my exit from this world, thus new worlds to find. We will not go quietly into the night, we will go quickly. Friends, au revoir.

STUNNED SILENCE AS CURTAIN CLOSES AND SHE RETURNS TO THE WINGS, A FEW CONFUSED CLAPS

CARSTAIRS Darling we can talk, after the show, you have to go on. Please.

SHE IS LEAVING, CARSTAIRS FOLLOWS HER OUT

XS There is no business like show business

XS TO ARCHIE Good night Archie. Thank you. (SHE IS GETTING INTO TAXI)

CARSTAIRS TO ARCHIE Thank you for what?

ARCHIE Let her go, Edward.

EXT ACOUSTIC - THE CAB DRIVES OFF. THERE IS A MOMENTARY SILENCE BETWEEN ARCHIE AND CARSTAIRS. THEN A CROWD IS BUILDING UP OUTSIDE THE THEATRE, SOME THEATRE GOERS ASKING FOR THEIR MONEY BACK, OTHERS SAYING TO EACH OTHER 'XS is right, Carstairs had a good run, all good things etc, Now what, can we bring the restaurant booking forward do you think….'

ARCHIE Ladies and Gentlemen, please, tonight's performance will continue as normal with an understudy standing in for XS

CARSTAIRS No one can stand in for XS

ARCHIE TO CARSTAIRS There isn't anything you can do here now. I'll call you a cab. TO THE CROWD Ladies and gentlemen, please…

CARSTAIRS I'll walk.

CARSTAIRS WALKS AS BEFORE ACROSS LONDON, SOUNDS MORE RAUCOUS THAN BEFORE, HE ACCIDENTLY WALKS INTO SOMEONE, HE SAYS 'I'm terribly sorry. THEY ARE RUDE TO HIM: 'Watch it, old man.' DIFFERENT CROWDS, MORE PUNK MUSIC. HE ARRIVES AT HIS CLUB.

DOOR Good evening, sir.

CARSTAIRS Is it?

DOOR You are a little earlier than usual, sir. I think a limited number of the first editions are in the bar.

CARSTAIRS ENTERS BAR

BAR MAN Your usual,sir?

CARSTAIRS What do you think man?

HE TAKES A DRINK, OPENS A NEWSPAPER, HE READS ALOUD

'The Drama Outside the Theatre by Brian Anderson

The most dramatic show in town tonight was actually outside the theatre. Minutes before curtain up on Edward Carstairs latest West End offering the theatre was hit by a lightning bolt from the blue more dramatic than anything in Lear, Hamlet or the Scottish play combined. Lady Sinclair addressed her adoring fans centre stage. She denounced the writer of the play, the West End legend Edward Carstairs as a has been. Announcing she no longer wished to be associated with the past, she immediately withdrew from the production. Her current whereabouts are unknown. What is known is she will not be returning to this or any other Carstairs production in the foreseeable future. The theatre has been besieged by theatre goers demanding refunds and the possibility the theatre may go dark must be entertained'.

CARSTAIRS (TO BARMAN) My good man, could you tell me when this edition was delivered?

BARMAN Must have been about 7.30 this evening sir. I understand it must be somewhat of a shock to you sir. Have this one on the house.

CARSTAIRS (CONTINUING READING) ‘As the theatre of the past was transferring from the West End to the street, the theatre of the future is happening South of the River, an explosion of words and energy in a new production by one to watch Pheobe Grace, a transfer from street to West End, a new era must be imminent.

(TO BARMAN, ACCEPTING DRINK) Thank you, most considerate.

10 – DAY INT ACOUSTIC –DIRECTOR'S OFFICE, ROYAL COURT THEATRE

TELEPHONE RINGS

LIONEL Director, Royal Court Theatre, the home of new writing

XS ON PHONE Anyone home?

LIONEL What?

XS Anyone home? You said Director, Royal court theatre, home of new writing

LIONEL XS?

XS Pheobe Grace. Did you leave your office, cross the river, descend your office in search of aforesaid new writing. Thought not. Bring her in again.

LIONEL I always thought it was a requirement of playwrights they could write dialogue.

XS Dialogue isn't everything. At the beginning. Stand her the bus fare. Invest. You don't want to look back on the wrong side of this.

LIONEL This what?

XS Maybe it is you who isn't listening or you only hear people who talk like you. You might have to change the way you answer the telephone. Get up with it. Hindsight is for dead people.

SHE RINGS OFF. LIONEL REDIALS. RINGING TONE FOR A WHILE.

GRACE ANSWERS ABOVE PUNK SONGS AND TYPING SOUND Pheobe Grace

LIONEL Miss Grace , do you mind if I call you Pheobe- I hope I'm not interrupting. This is Lionel Smart, Director Royal Court. Look we may have been somewhat short sighted with you over the bus fare…I see…yes, I hear you…I don't normally go south of…I mean we do normally expect prospective creatives to come in to Sloane Square. Well. Yes, no I do know where that is, I'm sure I can find it. Of course.

INT / EXT ACOUSTIC

DIRECTOR LEAVES ROYAL COURT TO CATCH BUS GOING SOUTH OF RIVER TO PERFORMANCE VENUE OF PHEOBE GRACE PLAY

BUS CONDUCTOR Hold tight, please, more room on top.

LIONEL So you actually do say that?

CONDUCTOR Come again, squire

LIONEL 'Hold tight please, more room on top'

CONDUCTOR Are you trying to be funny?

LIONEL No, I meant

CONDUCTOR Don't try to be funny. That will be 50p. To you.

LIONEL What will?

CONDUCTOR Your fare. What do you think?

LIONEL You don't know where I'm going.

CONDUCTOR I do. I 've had deck loads of your type on this route since…

LIONEL What type?

CONDUCTOR Not sure how to describe them. Theatrical types. Go out thoughtful, back very excited. I think you might have missed the bus.

THE BUS PROGRESSES SOUTH.

CONDUCTOR This, with great pleasure, is where I tell you where to get off.

DIRECTOR DESCENDS. TING TING OF BUS BELL AS IT DRIVES OFF. DIRECTOR ENTERS THE VENUE, AS HE OPENS THE DOOR HE IS MET WITH WALL OF PUNK MUSIC.

Y ABOVE THE NOISE Last time I saw you you were a walk out. We don't want any negative vibes here, man

LIONEL Where..

Y Some radio studio. One day you'll remember.

LIONEL Yes, I …

Y I've got to go and get ready. Lines to deliver.

THE VENUE FALLS SILENT. LIONEL LOOKING FOR SPACE.

LIONEL This seat taken?

BRI What do you want, a box?

SIR, XS Sit down, shut up and listen. SIR Sit here, we've been here every night so far but tonight we're leaving early doors. Not because you're here.

PLAY WITH PHEOBE AND Y RESUMES:

PHEOBE as X SETS SCENE A London bus, afternoon, south of the river, heading north

Y AS BUS CONDUCTOR You again, miss. Every time I see you, it's always the same. Notebook, window, notebook, window.

X All the world's a stage.

Y Or a stop. Where to, darling, you going all the way? Over the river, West End? Work, date, cinema?

X Theatre

Y Theatre, yeah I did have you down as creative type. You get all sorts of characters on my bus, upper deck, lower deck. Thought you might have been a musician. That's how young people seem to be expressing themselves these days. Writer, eh? Wouldn't mind a go at that myself, you hear and see all sorts of characters on my bus, upper deck, lower deck…

X Writing, what's stopping you? A full deck of excuses? Why don't you, have a go? Why…

PAUSE, THEN TUMULTOUS APPLAUSE CUT TO SWET AWARDS

XS It gives me pleasure beyond words to announce that Society of West End Theatre award this year for playwriting, most promising newcomer goes to (RIPS ENVELOPE) Pheobe Grace.

A FRAGMENT OF PUNK MUSIC IS PLAYED OVER THE APPLAUSE

XS Unfortunately Pheobe Grace cannot be with us this evening as she is busy writing and performing away from the West End. I am sure she will be gracing this platform in some other category countless times in the future. I accept this honour on her behalf. Thank you. And from one age to another, please welcome SIR to present the lifetime achievement award.

SIR Thank you XS. Most kind. First I would like to say how pleased I am that XS was able to accept the best newcomer award on behalf of Pheobe Grace. What could be more appropriate. By the theatrical laws of symmetry, the honour has befallen on me to represent the lifetime achievement award. For as long as I can remember, the talk of the town..

CUT TO INT TAXI

CABBIE ...talk of the town, a night at the Palladium, that's entertainment, back in the time when entertainment was entertainment, the west end was the best end, I remember taking the wife out for an anniversary, which one was it, paper, funnily enough, wouldn't take the wife there now mind you, what with all these, what do you call them, mohicans about, why doesn't the government do something, mind you Labour Party these days, apart from Denis pacifists, communists, this country, don't get me started, what we need is..

ARCHIE (IN BACK OF CAB) Will you stop talking. Please. Sorry. I don't mean to be rude. Stop talking and drive. Fast as traffic allows. I have someone very important to see.

CAB No offence meant governor, I'm entitled to my opinions same as the next man.

ARCHIE Put the radio on if silence is a problem for you. But put your foot down.

CUT TO SIR'S ORATION AT SWET

..a man who has given his life to theatre, to the craft of writing, an art some say is dying, but will never be dead as long as this man is lighting the way the way he has lit the great avenues of the West End of London for decades. For many of us here this evening, celebrating this lifetime of achievement, this man is our life in the theatre too. Actors, directors, producers, ASMs, the army behind the footlights that makes the magic happen, costumiers, make up, prompts, to the humblest of runners, sparks, chippies, stage door managers we have all been affected by the skill the towering contribution of this man, the

CUT TO TAXI, THE CABBIE IS SEARCHING THE AIRWAVES FOR SOMETHING ON THE RADIO, FRAGMENTS OF NEWS 'The Minister for Water Resources advises…' 'Mr Benn announced…' RADIO CRITICS 'We debate The State of British Theatre today..' MUSIC Wish You Were Here music by Pink Floyd, punk music by The Clash, SETTLES ON reggae

ARCHIE No not that. And keep driving. Very important, very important.

CABBIE EVENTUALLY SETTLES ON COATES' 'London Suite'

CABBIE More your style, sir?

CUT TO SIR NOW SPINNING THE SWET ORATION OUT

SIR I am speaking of course to our master of dialogue and stagecraft, the titan of theatre, that descendent of Maugham, Coward, perhaps even of the Bard himself…

BACK TO CABBIE STOPPING, END OF MUSIC AS ARCHIE JUMPS OUT SAYS TO CABBIE Keep the engine running. ARCHIE IS BANGING ON HOUSE DOOR

ARCHIE Edward, Mr Edward HE FORCES DOOR AND ENTERS FLAT. VERY LOUD PUNK MUSIC LOOPING ON RECORD PLAYER. Sir Edward. For God's sake , look at the state. HE MANAGES TO TURN OFF THE MUSIC.

CARSTAIRS (VERY DRUNK) Do you mind , I was listening to that?

ARCHIE White shirt, where is it?

CARSTAIRS I can't drink a shirt

ARCHIE It's black tie, someone has to keep up standards. We can have some caffeine there, now get in the cab. I said get in the cab now

CARSTAIRS I never really understood who you were , Archie

ARCHIE BUNDLES CARSTAIRS INTO THE WAITING CAB

ARCHIE TO CAB DRIVER Shaftesbury Avenue, Quick, direct. And quiet.

CAB TAKES OFF CUT TO SIR , RAMBLING NOW TO KEEP SWET GOING UNTIL TAXI ARRIVES WITH ARCHIE AND CARSTAIRS

SIR A man, who when all is said and done, is more than the sum of all his words, words that have brought him and given us riches in every sense, none more deserved. A man who know how to make an entrance, centre stage. A man who really needed no introduction, I give you for the Society of West End Theatre Lifetime Achievement Award, Edward Carstairs esq.

ARCHIE Cue

CARSTAIRS For?

ARCHIE Sir gave you the line ' I give you for the Society of West End Theatre Lifetime Achievement Award. Be gracious. Be big. Be you.

CARSTAIRS Ladies and Gentlemen HE HESITATES AND SEEMS LOST

BRI (NOT QUITE SOCE VOCE AT A FRONT OF HOUSE TABLE) He who hesitates is lost. Champagne, Edward, more champagne?

XS (TO BRI) Finish the champagne, Anderson, before I end you

CARSTAIRS Lady, Ladies and Gentlemen…and Brian Anderson. It is a profound honour (FINDING HIS MARK NOW) It is a profound honour to be the recipient of…

ARCHIE (PROMPT) The Society of West..

CARSTAIRS The Society of West End Theatre Lifetime Achievement Award. The acronym, I believe, SWET, most apposite, I'm sure this audience of all audiences will not want me to repeat the saw of inspiration and perspiration. Of course theatre isn't about ratios, it isn't about awards, lovely as recognition…

BRI …and money…

CARSTAIRS …is. As my predecessor said: 'all the world is a stage

SIR..you really have to hand it to him

XS Do you?

BRI Shut up

XS How dare you

SIR (TO XS ASIDE ABOUT BRI) How tiresome that little man is. How unrecognised he deserves to be.

CARSTAIRS …and all the men and women merely players. They have their exits and their entrances, and one man in his time plays many parts, his acts being seven stages.'

In my career so far in the bardic profession I have been blessed. Not only with talent, - it is some say the loneliest of occupations - but with companions on the path taken. I must mention Lady XS who has led me to where I am today, to SIR, the most stentorian and loyal of companions, to friends on and off stage, Archie you know who you are, and the constellation of stars around me too numerous to mention however luminous they know themselves to be. My life so far has, it is true been an achievement. My successes have brought me riches. I know I have through my words bought happiness to many and my words have at times bought happiness to me. I would like to share this honour this evening with Lady XS, who for once in this reversal of roles it is I the writer who call on the leading lady to join me centre stage

BRI SOTTO VOCE Will this never end?

XS AT HER FRONT OF HOUSE TABLE TO SIR Excuse me, I have some calls to make

AS SHE MAKES HER WAY OUT Excuse me, thank you, most kind, excuse me

CARSTAIRS NOTICES XS LEAVE BUT CONTINUES Exits and entrances, when and how, we can all learn whatever stage in our lifetime from Lady Xavier Sinclair the master, or is that the mistress of the art

XS NOW IN FOYER MAKING TELEPHONE CALL, PIPS.

I need to speak to the editor. No , I won't hold. I'll speak to him now.

CARSTAIRS CONTINUES TO AUDIENCE Writing is a lonely calling. Many of our bretheren, even those who will never feature in such an august gathering as the rather aptly named S W E T, have only Johnny Walker for company and no compensations. I have been blessed by the theatre Gods with, as I might put it , the best seat in the house. I have loved a beautiful woman….

XS IN FOYER ON PHONE I will only speak to the editor. Thank you. This is Lady Xavier Sinclair. It concerns Brian Anderson, your so called theatre critic. He has become the story. I want him to be history. Understand? Thank you. SHE REPLACES PHONE AND IS REDIALLING

Y ON A PAYPHONE, NOISY PUNK PARTY BACKGROUND Yeah, who is this?

CARSTAIRS CONTINUES IN HALL I have given and received, I have been loved by audiences the length of Shaftesbury Avenue, why stop there, the country, the continent, such is the universality of good writing, I have lived well from my art, but why the change of tense, playwrights have only one final curtain, one exit, recognition is not what I seek, though to receive this accolade is not without pleasure. Perhaps it is the end of an act, an interval, it is not the End. It may be timely, it is not time to accept this award. I might reconsider when I am dead. For now I thank you. I decline. I decline…

THERE IS SILENCE IN THE HALL.

ARCHIE LEAVES AND RUSHES TO FOYER, XS IS ON ANOTHER PHONE CALL

XS Put me through to the director of the Royal Court. I know he is there…

ARCHIE XS Please come quickly

XS He can't have finished his acceptance speech already, what is wrong with him?

THEY ARE RUSHING BACK INTO THE HALL

CARSTAIRS Thank you, Good evening, now if you will excuse me I have work to do.

HE IS COMING OFF THE ROSTRUM IN SILENCE

XS TO CARSTAIRS Darling, what is it?

CARSTAIRS Lifetime achievement award, some people have no sense of humour.

XS What have you done?

CARSTAIRS Declined.

XS BREAKS THE SILENCE BY BEGINNING TO APPLAUD.

11 - DAY INT XS WEST END FLAT

WHEN XS IS SPEAKING ON PHONE PALM COURT MUSIC LOW IN BACKGROUND, WHEN PHEOBE ON PHONE PUNK LOUD IN BACKGROUND.

XS ON PHONE Miss Grace, I do assure you I tried to phone you but couldn't get through. You do seem to operate in an high volume environment.

PHEOBE You haven't spoken to me. Who did you speak to?

XS A young lady, gave her name as Y. Said she would speak to you. It seems to have been a rather chaotic night all round. Look I would really rather speak to you in person. No, I don't do buses. You come here. I'll send a car. We will be expecting you.

REPLACES PHONE, MUSIC STOPS

12 – SAME DAY AND LOCATION LATER

XS Archie, be a dear and mix me a drink

ARCHIE I don't do drinks.

CARSTAIRS I'll fix the drinks.

ARCHIE Let's do this without drinks.

DOOR OPENS, PHEOBE ENTERS

XS I'll do introductions. Dramatis Personae. Or do we all know each other by now…

CARSTAIRS TO PHEOBE I'll fix your script. Edward Carstairs.

PHEOBE I'll fix yours, you never were zeitgeist were you? Au fond. Pheobe Grace.

XS Darlings, let's start at the beginning. Where all good theatre stories start. Contracts

PHEOBE I have a contract. Royal Court. You didn't get through, come through in time, estimate you were about 40 years too late.

XS Young lady , you have a lot to learn

PHEOBE Who from? You ?

XS Contracts are ink. In this business

PHEOBE Business?

XS / CARSTAIRS TOGETHER In this business

CARSTAIRS I'm sorry darling, do finish your sentence

XS In this business, ink is money. We can write the Royal Court out of the picture.

PHEOBE I signed a contract.

XS Let me assure you we can sort out the contract. You are the talent. You can make money.

PHEOBE I don't need money

XS My dear, you do. Play your pages right, I mean more money than you can imagine. We aren't talking bus fares home, we aren't talking taxis, we are talking limos, stretch limo, Rockstar limos.

PHEOBE You are talking sell out.

XS Exactly. A sell out every night for the rest of your professional life. Which starts now. Archie. The plan. Listen. Learn, Earn.

ARCHIE There is a window

CARSTAIRS A window? Not sure I follow you man.

XS Shut up, Edward

ARCHIE There is a window at the Apollo. Since Edward's last

CARSTAIRS flop?

PHEOBE Shut up, Sir Edward Carstairs.

ARCHIE The Apollo has gone dark. They want to open in 7 weeks time with a new hit

SIR What is this Juke Box Jury?

CARSTAIRS Shut up, SIR

ARCHIE A new hit with new writing, a play for today, not telly, small screen, big stage, theatre is back. It never went away, we did. Or to be more blunt, or sharp, some of you, naming no names Sir Edward, went away, XS came back in time, so did Sir Edward at the SWET awards. This is curtain up, not the final curtain.

SIR Life isn't a rehearsal.

ARCHIE Shut up, all of you, until you have something original to say. Pheobe and Y are right, music may be the future now, words and music, a new rhythm,

PHEOBE A reggae musical?

ARCHIE I didn't expect stereotyping from you. And it's been done, but we are open to all ideas. New ideas, or new old ideas.

CARSTAIRS We?

ARCHIE The Apollo has a window in 10 weeks time. You, Edward and Pheobe are going to be locked in a room, I don't mean a green room, or 100 or Garrick club , until you have written the hit, a hit with integrity, meaning, relevance and above all, dialogue. A script. A masterpiece.

SIR Can it be done?

ARCHIE I'm glad you said that as a question, rather than a statement. You're in. So we have a main cast – we'll need more, Pheobe, your area. Writers – Carstairs and Grace

PHEOBE Grace and Carstairs

ARCHIE Producer, XS

CARSTAIRS Director?

ARCHIE Me

CARSTAIRS You?

ARCHIE I was the leading director in Jamaica before I got on the Windrush.

The rest I learned at the stage door of the Apollo. If you want to see a CV right now I think it'll be me asking for yours rather than vice-versa. I want you and Pheobe back here tomorrow with ideas, themes, plots. I mean theatre plots. 9 A M.

13- LATE SAME EVENING/ EARLY MORNING INT XS FLAT, CARSTAIRS AND PHEOBE ALL NIGHTER BRAINSTORM SESSION

CARSTAIRS Have you ever been up this early before?

PHEOBE Have you ever been up this late?

CARSTAIRS You know Archie may have this wrong you know, not impossible.

PHEOBE I trust him, there is something about him. What do you think he might be wrong about?

CARSTAIRS Me and you

PHEOBE What about me and you?

CARSTAIRS Opposites. We aren't that different. Au fond.

PHEOBE Meaning

CARSTAIRS Au fond…

PHEOBE If you can't overcome your addiction

CARSTAIRS Addiction?

PHEOBE To being patronising, to your self believing monopoly on writing skills, to..I'm too tired for lists. I would like Archie to be right. If it is possible let's make it work. Look, I'll make it easier for you, concede you have better West End writing skills…

CARSTAIRS Used to. You have better South End writing skills

PHEOBE So let's make us work, prove Archie right, be complementary.

CARSTAIRS So what have you got, ideas, short list.

PHEOBE What have you got? Thought so. Need a drink? Want to go to your club?

CARSTAIRS Want to go to yours?

PHEOBE At least they let women in. We've been up all night, what have you got?

CARSTAIRS I can write. I don't have to prove that.

PHEOBE This isn't about writing. Yet. It's about ideas.

CARSTAIRS You don't seem to have any either. Any idea.

PHEOBE I know. How to find them. Hold tight please, you seem like a top deck kind of guy.

14 EARLY MORNING EXT -INT ACOUSTIC

BUS CROSSING THE THAMES SOUTH TO NORTH.

BUS CONDUCTOR Shaftesbury Avenue. All change please. TO PHEOBE Nice to see you again, Miss, I'm glad you found a companion to travel with other than your notebook. Good morning to you, sir

CARSTAIRS Good morning. Thank you.

THEY DISEMBARK, BUS TURNS ROUND AND DRIVES BACK SOUTH, PHEOBE AND CARSTAIRS ENTER APOLLO THEATRE BY STAGE DOOR. THE NEW STAGE DOOR MANAGER IS THE FORMER DIRECTOR OF ROYAL COURT, LIONEL

LIONEL Good morning Miss Grace, Sir Edward, Archie is expecting you in the green room. I expect you know the way. Sir.

PHEOBE Nice to see you opening the door to new talent. What's the story here?

CARSTAIRS We don't have time for this now Pheobe. Break a leg.

THEY ASCEND STAIRS AND ENTER THE GREEN ROOM

ARCHIE What have you got?

CARSTAIRS Good morning Archie

ARCHIE If you can't do this tell me right now. I can bring other people in. Pheobe, what ...

PHEOBE ...We've got is a number of scenarios.

ARCHIE I thought we'd eliminated the reggae musical. Next.

PHEOBE A minor politician finds herself at the centre of political power as a government loses its overall majority and she is approached to support policies she doesn't really agree with in order to win advantages for her south London constituents.

ARCHIE Thank you. Next.

PHEOBE An early warning radar station detects a nuclear missile is about to hit an English city. There has been insufficient time to prepare an evacuation plan, a secret committee is formed to select those who can be evacuated and those who will remain in the blast zone.

ARCHIE I am not sure of your commercial theatre sense, sister. Next. You did say you were up all night, what were you doing?

PHEOBE During a prolonged period of drought gangs form to deal in water at vastly inflated prices, cites become divided by dams, those who control water live more lavish lifestyles than those who control oil.

ARCHIE A veritable deluge of ideas my dear, Carstairs seems rather a washout. Edward?

CARSTAIRS A lonely man on the top deck of a bus befriends a woman on the lower deck. They exchange stories and reminisce as bus stops become memory prompts of brief encounters.

ARCHIE Who is going to buy a ticket to that one? The meter is ticking. Come back tomorrow, this is a west end theatre, a big stage, I want ideas that fill it. Sleep is optional for you, I don't want it to be mandatory for the audience.

15 - EARLY THE NEXT   EXT DAY

BUSES ARRIVING AT SHAFTESBURY AVENUE

CARSTAIRS AND PHEOBE DISEMBARK FROM RESPECTIVE BUSES

CONDUCTOR TO PHEOBE Perhaps you should think about a season ticket?

PHEOBE Perhaps I'll buy you one.

CONDUCTOR Where's the old man this morning?

CARSTAIRS LEAVING HIS BUS, TO PHEOBE So it's true about two buses arriving at once

PHEOBE And it's true about working on the buses? Don't you think?

MEET UP OUTSIDE THE APOLLO, THEY ENTER STAGE DOOR - INT

LIONEL TO PHEOBE AND CARSTAIRS I've heard of separate tables, what are you going to call this one separate buses?

PHEOBE Don't give up the day job

CARSTAIRS He may be onto something there. Need to work on the title. Double Decker?

PHEOBE Hold Tight Please?

THEY WALK BRISKLY UPSTAIRS CARSTAIRS SLIGHTLY OUT OF BREATH

CARSTAIRS Not as young as I used to be

PHEOBE We'll work on the title when we have a script. Right way round.

THEY ENTER GREEN ROOM

ARCHIE What have you got?

PHEOBE AND CARSTAIRS TOGETHER Good morning Archie

CARSTAIRS Ladies first

PHEOBE Ever the gent

ARCHIE What is this, The good companions? What have you…

PHEOBE We've got –

CARSTAIRS We have –

PHEOBE A synopsis

ARCHIE Sounds nasty. Let's hear it…Pheobe

PHEOBE London, mid 1970s, Britain's leading playwright premieres yet another hit.

But fashions are changing, in fashion, in music, in politics, and in the West End. Stars may shine most brightly before they implode, how do those who are living in success know an era is ending?

CARSTAIRS Synopsis, Pheobe dear.

PHEOBE In the city the cultural epicentre is shifting form West and North to South and East.

As songs shift from triple album length to three minutes, theatre moves for three act two glass Bordeaux interval to contemporary one act plays. The playwright cannot change in time, the theatre he supports goes dark, new work is emerging mirroring the music scene. A chance meeting sees the new sharp raw writing collide with the stagecraft of yesteryear to produce, quite literally a new tomorrow. The two talents team up, bypass the traditional outlets for new writing, even those who believe themselves new are old, and a new vital form renews the traditional theatre for the now generation.

ARCHIE What have you got?

PHEOBE I just told you

CARSTAIRS He means story , darling.

ARCHIE You might have something. I want a scene for the third act by day after tomorrow

PHEOBE Impossible

CARSTAIRS Come on Phoebe, let's start, get this show on the road right now.

PHEOBE Do you want me to fail?

CARSTAIRS Us

PHEOBE Is this a plan, a west end plan?

THEY ARE LEAVING THE THEATRE, WALKING ALONG SHAFTESBURY AVENUE

CARSTAIRS No this is A BUS STOPS THEY GET ON, UPPER DECK

CONDUCTOR Where to, guv?

CARSTAIRS Circular, we want a ticket back to where we started. Let's work. Top deck.

16 - DAY INT THE DAY AFTER TOMORROW, THE REHEARSAL ROOM AT APOLLO THEATRE

LIONEL TO ARCHIE Can they do it?

ARCHIE Do you want them to? CARSTAIRS AND PHEOBE ARRIVE What have you got?

CARSTAIRS AND PHEOBE READ FROM THEIR SCRIPT:

CARSTAIRS What is that?

PHEOBE It's a suitcase

CARSTAIRS I can see that

PHEOBE So why have you asked?

CARSTAIRS What does it represent?

PHEOBE It's a suitcase. It doesn't represent anything

CARSTAIRS Do you know what your problem is?

PHEOBE Is there a problem?

CARSTAIRS Yes. Do you know what it is?

PHEOBE No

CARSTAIRS You are too literal.

PHEOBE You used to like me

CARSTAIRS You're not listening

PHEOBE I haven't time

CARSTAIRS You haven't time?

PHEOBE I have a train to catch

CARSTAIRS So that's it.

PHEOBE That's what.

CARSTAIRS That's why you have the suitcase

PHEOBE I have the suitcase because I have a train to catch?

CARSTAIRS Is this conversation going anywhere?

PHEOBE The conversation might not be. I am.

CARSTAIRS Where?

PHEOBE Shouldn't the first question be why?

CARSTAIRS That's the last question

PHEOBE I have to go

CARSTAIRS Why?

PHEOBE Why?

CARSTAIRS Is there only one train? Catch the next. The one after the next. Please.

PHEOBE Don't you get it

CARSTAIRS I'd prefer it if you didn't-

IN THIS SENTENCE THE READ THROUGH PART PLAYED BY CARSTAIRS BECOMES PLAYED BY SIR AND THE PART BY PHEOBE BECOMES PLAYED BY XS IN FULL PERFORMANCE ON STAGE AT THE OPENING NIGHT OF THE APOLLO THEATRE-

SIR I'd prefer it if you stay.

XS The suitcase is packed.

SIR Do you have to be so literal?

XS Do you have to be so literary. It took me a long time to pack that suitcase.

SIR Of course. You are being metaphorical. You put one thing in, then another, then…God, it's heavy do you want me to help you?

XS To go?

SIR Tell you what, sit down, have a drink, I'll help you. To unpack it. Take everything out. I'll change. You won't be able to fill it up again. Promise.

XS Sit down, have a drink, fill it up, promise. I 've heard it all before.

SIR I don't want you to go.

XS That's why I'm going. If I stay any longer it will be too late.

SIR I'll put some music on. Your choice. You used to love that.

XS Yes, used to. Now it's silence. The wrong kind.

SIR It is always easier to go than stay. I'm not impressed. It isn't heroic.

XS I didn't say it was. It's time.

SIR Come on, music that's the answer. You choose. Vinyl. This seems like a vinyl kind of moment. Your choice. Yes, I'll choose something from your collection, those songs you used to play, windows open, a May evening, remember – should I stay or should I go, thin line between love and hate, I didn't mean to hurt you…

XS The hits just keep on coming…

SIR … Ain't too proud to beg, cracked actor…let me see, you used to keep them here. We'll have a party. We'll have a ball. You used to keep them here. What…where…Oh I see. Open the suitcase. Please.

XS Don't say old times sake.

SIR Open the suitcase. Your choice. Totally. Your choice, make it a LP , not a single, both sides. Triple album, box set, something that goes on a very long time.

XS You said it was my choice.

/

XS CLICKS OPEN THE SUITCASE AND TAKES OUT A RECORD, WALKS OVER TO THE RECORD PLAYER. THERE IS THE HISS OF OLD VINYL, THE CLASH 'SHOULD STAY OR SHOULD I GO' STARTS. THEY LISTEN. SIR BREAKS IN

SIR Darling…

XS Listen, why don't you listen

THE SONG CONTINUES

SIR Metaphor

XS Rhetoric

CURTAIN
MOMENTARY SILENCE IN THE AUDITORIUM

Y SOTTO VOCE IN AUDITORIUM Classic. SHE BEGINS TO WHOOP, CHEER AND CLAP

ARCHIE SOTTO VOCE IN AUDITORIUM My God, I think they've done it

THE APPLAUSE BUILDS IN THE THEATRE, A COMBINATION OF OLD STYLE WEST END CLAPPING AND NEW STYLE WHOOPS AND CHEERS.

BBC CRITIC CHAIR AS REPORTER IN AUDITORIUM The West End hasn't seen or heard a night like it since…HE IS LOST IN THE APPLAUSE

SIR AND XS TAKING CURTAIN CALLS AND COMING INTO WINGS OFFSTAGE TO MEET CARSTAIRS AND PHEOBE

SIR You two take the applause, it's for you.

CARSTAIRS TO PHEOBE It's for you

PHEOBE Writers don't go on stage.

CARSTAIRS Quite right, always know when to get off.

XS Indeed. So where to now?

SIR Club?

PHEOBE I know exactly the place

CARSTAIRS Lead on

THE APPLAUSE OF THE THEATRE IS REPLACED BY THE ROAR OF PUNK ROCK CLUB

SILENCE

THEATRE / RADIO CREDITS 'BROADCAST' OVER THE SOUNDS OF CAST IN THE CLUB

SIGN OFF BY BBC ANNOUNCER…And the award for best newcomers goes to…

West End Story

JK 2017

ISBN 9780993130657

Also by **John F King** at **York Europe Publishing:**

Wise Guy and other fables, 2008

ISBN 978-0-955851902

Wise Guy, 2012, is also available as an eBook at

Smashwords ISBN 9781476351735

***Drama King**, 2010

ISBN 978-0-955851919

Funky / Guy and other micro-fiction, 2012

ISBN 978-0-955851964

Micro-Waves, 2012

ISBN 978-0-955851933

Vienna, Love, 2014

ISBN 978-0-955851971

Write Coach, 2014

ISBN 978-0-955851988

Write Coach II 2015

ISBN 978-0-9931306-1-8

A and E 2014

ISBN 978-0-955851995

Prog 2015

ISBN 978-0-9931306-0-1

What's Left 2016

ISBN 978-0-993106-2-5

Low – Rise 2016

ISBN 978-0-9931306-3-2

SW10

ISBN 978-0-9931306-4-9

John F King has completed writing courses at

Artworks

Arvon

City Lit London

Edx

JBW London

NCTJ

Oxford University Department for Continuing Education

Script Yorkshire

Skyros Writers' Lab

UCLA (online), UEA / Future Learn (online)

York University Centre for Lifelong Learning

www.johnkinginternational.eu

West End Story

ISBN 978-0-9931306-5-6

London / York 2018

West End Story

By

John F King

York Europe Publishing
2017

ISBN 9780993130656

www.johnkinginternational.eu

www.ingramcontent.com/pod-product-compliance
Ingram Content Group UK Ltd.
Pitfield, Milton Keynes, MK11 3LW, UK
UKHW060121300726
14090UKWH00002B/293
* 9 7 8 0 9 9 3 1 3 0 6 5 6 *